Chapter One

'TODAY,' SAID MISS Harrison, 'we're going to learn about the sorts of things that animals eat. In particular, we're going to find out about something called a food chain. What are we going to find out about, class?'

'A food chain!' the children shouted back.

'Good,' said Miss Harrison. 'Who can suggest an animal to start with?'

'A polar bear, Miss!' Tommy Fegan said.

'Very good,' said Miss Harrison. 'Do you know what polar bears eat, Tommy?'

Tommy shook his head.

'Never mind,' said Miss Harrison, 'let's ask our polar bear expert, shall we?' She looked at Billy Cockcroft. Everybody knew that the polar bear was Billy's favourite animal.

'Billy, what do polar bears eat?'

Miss Harrison tapped her foot and waited for Billy to answer. But Billy was almost nodding off. He'd stayed up late, playing his brand new CD-Rom the night before. It was called *The Frozen North* and it showed lots of interesting things about the Arctic. If you clicked on the correct piece of snow or ice, a bear called Lorel popped out of his den and talked about the freezing Arctic climate.

Right at that moment, the climate was getting rather chilly in the classroom. Miss Harrison was beginning to lose her patience . . .

'Wake up, Billy!' she clapped.

Billy jumped in surprise. Miss Harrison frowned at him. 'What are we learning, today?' she asked sternly.

Billy bit his lip. He hadn't got a clue. He looked at his best friend, Josie Westacott. Josie tried to whisper something but Billy couldn't hear her properly.

'Food trains, Miss?' he tried.

The whole class sniggered. Josie covered her face.

'Food chains,' Miss Harrison tutted crossly. 'We are trying to find out what a polar bear eats. Tonight, Mr Sleepyhead, I would like you to find out something about the polar bear's food chain. You can tell the class all about it tomorrow.'

'Yes, Miss Harrison,' Billy mumbled.

Just then, the classroom door burst open. A chubby little man with a pencil behind one ear staggered in carrying a large cardboard box.

'Delivery,' he puffed. 'Where shall I put it?'

'On my desk, please,' Miss Harrison beamed.

'Miss, what is it?' the children shouted.

The delivery man winked. He put the box down and slid it round. Written across the side was the word COMPUTER . . .

Chapter Two

'ANOTHER COMPUTER?' BILLY'S mum said, as she put two bowls of spaghetti on the table. 'Goodness, you'll be going to the moon next.'

'It's brilliant,' said Josie, who had come to tea. 'It's got much better software than the other computers. We're going to be on the Internet. That means we can look up all sorts of things.'

'And send letters,' Billy put in, twirling a

strand of spaghetti round his fork.

'Letters?' said Mrs Cockcroft doubtfully.

'You know, e-mail,' Josie explained.

Mrs Cockcroft hummed. 'Well I think I'll stick with good old-fashioned snail mail, the kind you put in a post-box, thank you. Internet, indeed. You'll be telling me it makes cups of tea next.'

'It's got a CD-Rom drive,' Billy said excitedly, 'so I'll be able to take *The Frozen North* to school.' That reminded him – about Miss Harrison's homework.

'Mum,' he said, 'what's a food chain?'

'One with polar bears in it,' Josie added.

'A food chain?' Mrs Cockcroft repeated. 'It's what you call a line of supermarkets, isn't it?'

Josie wrinkled her nose. 'I don't think so,' she muttered, looking at Billy. 'I've never seen a bear in a supermarket, have you?'

Just then, Billy's dad walked in. He said hello to Josie, gave his wife a kiss, tousled Billy's hair and switched the TV on. Mr Cockcroft liked to watch the evening news while he was eating his tea.

'What's a food chain, Dad?' Billy asked at once.

Mr Cockcroft grinned. 'It's what you get if you tie some spaghetti together.'

Billy and Josie laughed. Mrs Cockcroft didn't. Something on the television had caught her eye.

9

'Ooh,' she said, 'a polar bear.'

'Where?' said Billy, turning to look.

Sure enough, there on the TV news was a polar bear. It was pacing restlessly across the ice, shaking its paws as if it were trying to throw something off. Billy frowned and leaned in closer to the set. The polar bear's paws were a funny colour. So was the ice it was walking on. So were all the animals lying on the ice. Billy recognised them now. They were Arctic Seals. Seals, he knew, were normally greyish-white. But these seals were black, slimy jet black.

Suddenly, the TV picture changed.

It showed an oil tanker far out to sea. The ship was broken and lurching on its side. Oil was spilling from a hole in its hull. Huge sheets of oil were spreading across the ocean and lapping ashore. Then Billy realised what was wrong – the ice and the animals were covered in oil.

'This is the worst environmental disaster the Arctic has ever seen,' said a newscaster. 'The cost of cleaning up the oil is estimated at many millions of pounds. The cost to local wildlife is already very much higher than that.'

Josie shuddered and turned her face away as the TV showed evidence of dead seabirds, drenched in oil. Even Mr Cockcroft gulped uneasily. Just then, the newscaster said: 'Experts fear that the Arctic food chain could be broken . . .'

'What?' cried Billy.

'Come on,' said Mr Cockcroft, patting Billy's arm, 'finish your tea. There's nothing you can do.'

Billy frowned. There ought to be something he could do for those animals. He twirled some spaghetti rather sadly round his fork, ate one more mouthful then pushed his dish away. Suddenly, he didn't feel hungry any more.

Chapter Three

WHEN JOSIE HAD gone, Billy went upstairs
to play *The Frozen North*. He was hoping to
learn about the polar bear's food chain, but
somehow he couldn't concentrate. He clicked
rather wearily around the screen and even
yawned a couple of times. Soon, he
abandoned the computer altogether and
trudged downstairs to get a drink of water.
But he couldn't stop thinking about the bear
and the oil. What had the newscaster meant
when he'd said: 'The Arctic food chain could
be broken?' Billy sighed and went to sit in the

garden. He wished someone could explain it to him.

Just then, something peculiar happened: a few snowflakes started to fall and the air turned very misty and cold. Billy lifted his beaker to take a drink of water . . . only to find his water had frozen! The next he knew there was ice all around him. Suddenly, something came out of the mist. Something large and white with rounded ears and a big black nose. Great puffs of polar breath were blowing from its jaws. It was Lorel, the bear from *The Frozen North!*

'It's you!' cried Billy.

'Is it?' said Lorel.

'Yes,' Billy nodded. 'How did you get here?'

'Don't know,' said the bear.

'It doesn't matter,' said Billy. 'Have *you* come to tell me about food chains and the oil?'

'Probably,' said the bear, looking a bit bemused. 'Is that what this smelly black stuff is?' He lifted up a paw. It was covered in oil.

'Yes,' said Billy, having a sniff.

'I don't suppose you know how to get it off?'

Billy thought he did. 'Hang on,' he said.

'What to?' asked Lorel, looking around.

But Billy had already dashed into the kitchen. He had often seen his dad scrub oil off his hands. He used washing-up liquid and a stiff nail brush. Billy didn't think a tiddly nail brush would be much use on a polar bear. So he ran to the cupboard for the yard brush instead. Then he squirted some Sudso into the washing-up bowl and filled the bowl with bubbly water. He carried the bowl and the brush outside.

'Lie down,' said Billy. Lorel flopped onto his tummy. Billy dipped the brush in the soapy water and started scrubbing Lorel's fur!

Soon the oil began to come off. Billy had to scrub hard, but Lorel didn't mind. He seemed to be enjoying every minute of it!

'Left a bit,' he said, wiggling his bottom. 'Up a bit. Stop. There! Scrub there!'

'Apart from being so messy,' Billy puffed, 'what's so bad about all that oil?'

The bear rolled on his back with his paws in the air. 'It sticks to your fur when you swim in it,' he said, 'and if you try to lick it off, it gives you a tummy-ache! The fish don't like it; it poisons them. And if the seals eat the fish, it poisons them, too! Do you think you could scrub my tummy now?'

Billy blew a sigh and clambered up the bear's side. 'So, has someone got to scrub the fish clean?' he said. That would be difficult. Even with a nail brush.

'No,' said the bear. 'I'm afraid the fish die.'

'But if they die,' said Billy, 'the seals won't have any good fish to eat – then they'll die.'

'I know,' said the bear, his great tummy rumbling, 'and then we won't have any seals to eat.'

'But then you'll die, too!' Billy exclaimed.

'Quite,' said the bear. 'I think you missed a bit under my chin.'

Billy did the bear's chin and jumped down quickly. 'This is terrible,' he said. 'I'm going to tell Miss Harrison about it.'

'Good idea,' said the bear. 'Tell everyone you know.'

'I will,' Billy said. 'I might write to my MP – that's what Dad always says we should do. I might send a letter on the school computer!'

'I should,' said the bear, though he hadn't the foggiest idea what an MP, a letter or a computer were.

'If you're hungry now, I could run and ask Mum to cook you something?' Billy said.

'Seal?' said the bear, with a hopeful look.

Billy shook his head. 'I think seals are too big to fit in the freezer. We've got fish-fingers! I can get you some of those!' And he ran into the kitchen to have a look.

That was where his mum caught up with him. 'Billy,' she said, tapping his shoulder, 'what are you doing? Close that freezer.'

'I'm getting some food for the bear!' explained Billy.

Mrs Cockcroft looked puzzled. 'Bear? What bear?'

Billy pointed to the garden – but apart from the faintest dusting of snow, Lorel and the ice had completely disappeared.

'Come on,' said Mrs Cockcroft, 'upstairs to bed – and don't forget to switch that computer off, please.'

Billy scratched his head. He was sure he'd seen a bear. It had told him things about the food chain, hadn't it? He trudged upstairs a bit confused. On the computer, his snowflake screensaver had started up. He nudged the mouse and a scene from *The Frozen North* appeared. It was Lorel, the ice bear, sitting there, waiting. Billy clicked on Lorel's nose.

'Don't forget what I told you,' Lorel whispered – and the program shut down.

Chapter Four

AT SCHOOL THE next day, everyone was talking about the oil spill.

'Calm down, class,' Miss Harrison said. 'We *will* do something to help the animals.' She turned to Billy: 'You did well to find out about the fish and the seals, Billy. Your CD-Rom sounds very interesting. It's quite useful, being able to talk to a bear! He seems to have told you a lot about the food chain.'

The class began to giggle. Miss Harrison smiled. She turned to the board and drew four pictures – some tiny things called plankton, a fish, a seal, and a tubby polar bear.

'This is the polar bear's food chain,' she said, drawing a line between each picture. 'The bears survive by eating the seals, the seals eat the fish, the fish eat the plankton. But if an accident should cause even the plankton to die, it can affect all the other animals higher up the chain.'

She rubbed out the fish and drew a sorry face on the seal. Then she rubbed out the seal and drew an even sorrier face on the bear.

'An oil spill can make this happen. We say it breaks the chain.'

'But, Miss, what can we do?' asked Josie.

'Two things,' said Miss Harrison. 'First, we can write to the leaders of the oil-producing nations and tell them how concerned we are about the effect oil spills have on the environment. Secondly, we can raise some money to send to the Arctic Wildlife Appeal!'

The children cheered. Billy raised his hand.

'How are we going to do it, Miss?'

'Ah,' said Miss Harrison, 'your polar bear has given me a rather good idea . . .'

Chapter Five

'A SPONSORED SCRUB!' Mrs Cockcroft hooted. 'That'll be the day! I have to chase you into the bath as it is!'

'Not *us*, Mum,' said Billy. 'We're scrubbing a rug.'

'A rug?' said Mrs Cockcroft. 'Whatever for?'

'It's a white one,' said Josie, 'like a polar bear's fur. Miss Harrison's going to spill oil all over it and we're going to scrub it off – 50p for five minutes. Will you sponsor me, please? You have to sign this bit of paper.'

'Me too,' said Billy, 'I'm going to do an hour!'

Mrs Cockcroft scratched her head. 'Well, it's an odd way to raise money, I must say. Still, it is a good cause. Brian, sponsor them!'

'What?' said Mr Cockcroft, nearly choking on his tea. Billy pushed the sponsor form under his dad's nose.

'It's for the polar bears, Dad. We can save them if we send money quickly to help clean the oil from their fur.'

Mr Cockcroft winced. 'Can't you write a letter to your MP instead?'

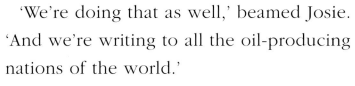

'We're doing that as well,' beamed Josie.
'And we're writing to all the oil-producing
nations of the world.'

'On the new computer,' Billy said.

Mrs Cockcroft nodded at her husband.
'There,' she said proudly, 'the new computer.'

'All right, put me down for a fiver,' Mr
Cockcroft sighed.

Chapter Six

THE SPONSORED SCRUB was a huge success.
Josie got twelve sponsors; Billy got eleven.
He asked everyone he knew, including the
milkman, the postman and a man who came
to sell brushes at the door. Even Mr Gribble,
Billy's grumpy next door neighbour, signed
up for two whole pounds worth of scrubbing
– but only on the understanding that Billy
would wash his car as well.

29

The scrub was done on a Saturday morning. All the parents came to watch. A reporter came too, from the Ruffley Gazette. She took pictures of the children holding scrubbing brushes in one hand and washing-up bottles in the other! Billy thought he saw a man with a video camera, but he didn't pay it much attention.

At ten o'clock precisely, Miss Harrison uncurled the rug in the playground. Mr Creekmore, the head teacher, splashed it with oil. Everyone shouted, 'Boo!' Miss Harrison put a whistle to her lips.

'Ready?' she shouted. The children cheered. Miss Harrison blew – and the scrubbing began!

It was very hard work – worse than scrubbing a bear, Billy thought. By the time Miss Harrison blew the whistle again, he felt as if his arms were about to drop off. Mr Creekmore got a hose and washed the soap suds away. The parents clapped, but most of the children had very long faces. There were still a lot of oily patches on the rug.

Oddly enough, Miss Harrison seemed pleased. She turned the children to face their parents. 'Thank you for sponsoring our scrubbers!' she said. 'Please note, despite their hard work, the rug is still oily. This is to show

just how difficult it can be to clean up an oil spill! Imagine this was a polar bear's fur!'

The parents looked impressed.

'So!' Miss Harrison announced firmly. 'We are now going to write to all the oil-producing countries to express our concern, aren't we class?'

'Yes!' they chorused – and rushed into the classroom.

Everyone wanted to be first to the computer – to watch Miss Harrison type the message in!

Chapter Seven

'THIS COMPUTER,' MISS Harrison said, with twenty-six goggle-eyed children around her, 'is able to send electronic messages to other computers all over the world. First we have to type an address – like this:'

president@whitehouse.usa

'The White House is where the President of America lives; usa stands for United States of America. The funny squiggle means "at". So we're sending our message to the President at his home in America.'

'Are we really writing to America?' gasped Josie.

'Not just America,' Miss Harrison stressed. 'We'll be sending the same letter to all the countries that transport oil. This is just an example. Watch!'

Dear Mr President, Miss Harrison typed,
The staff and children of Ruffley Primary School, Ruffley Park, England, wish to express their deep concern about the oil spill in the Arctic. We are shocked at the sight of polluted coastlines and the suffering inflicted on local wildlife. We would like your assurance that your government will be doing everything in its power to prevent such a disaster ever happening again, in the hope that future generations will still have some wildlife left to enjoy.
Yours sincerely,
Miss Julia Harrison (teacher)

'Ready?' said Miss Harrison.

The children nodded. Miss Harrison clicked the mouse. The computer beeped.

Message sent, it reported. And everyone cheered.

On Monday morning, the first replies arrived. The new computer beeped three times during Miss Harrison's talk on recycling. The children could barely contain their excitement.

'Slowly!' she thundered, when she finally allowed them up to her desk. When everyone was settled, Miss Harrison clicked on the e-mail folder. The children gasped as a message flashed up. It said:

Thank you for mailing the Kremlin. The Russian President has been informed of your comments.

'Is that it?' said Josie. A groan of disappointment echoed round the class – especially as the replies from Kuwait and Canada said much the same thing.

Miss Harrison sighed. 'World leaders are very busy people,' she said. 'We mustn't expect too much, too soon. Besides, we did raise three hundred and seventy two pounds from our sponsored scrub. That's going to help save some animals, isn't it? What's more,

I thought we might e-mail other schools and tell them about our scrub-a-rug idea to see if they want to try it themselves.'

Everyone thought that was a brilliant idea, and the computer was beeping like mad all

afternoon as e-mail messages whizzed back and forth. The class were really enjoying themselves. No one wanted school to finish that day, until Miss Harrison mysteriously announced:

'One last thing. I want you all to watch the local evening news tonight. You might see something very interesting . . .'

When Billy's dad came home that night the TV set was already on. Billy was watching a news report, all about the Arctic Wildlife Appeal. It showed seabirds having their feathers cleaned, then being released far away from the oil.

'It is a mammoth task,' the reporter was saying, 'and the clean-up will continue for

many months yet. But thanks to the efforts of local children, like these at Ruffley Park Primary School, countless lives have already been saved.' Suddenly, the TV picture changed and Billy almost fell off his seat. His class was on the television – doing their sponsored scrub!

'Looks fun, doesn't it?' the reporter chuckled. 'This chap certainly isn't complaining . . .'

Billy bit his lip. His eyes went very moist.
On the screen now was a real polar bear. He
was lying on the ice, fast asleep it seemed,
while a man scrubbed the oil off his fur. Now
Billy knew that he and his class really had
done something to help the animals –
something good, something special,
something magical almost.

And the magic didn't end there.

Later that night, Billy went upstairs to play *The Frozen North*. The computer was on and the snowflake screensaver had started up. Billy sat down and nudged the mouse. The snowflake pattern didn't disappear. Billy hit the keyboard. Still the snowflakes tumbled down. Billy tutted and was just about to call his dad, when the snowflakes began to form a message:

Well done, Billy
we're proud of you!

and underneath was the sender's address

Lorel@frozen.north

Yellow Bananas are bright, funny, brilliantly imaginative stories written by some of today's top writers. All the books are beautifully illustrated in full colour.

So if you've enjoyed this story, why not pick another one from the bunch?

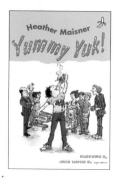